The

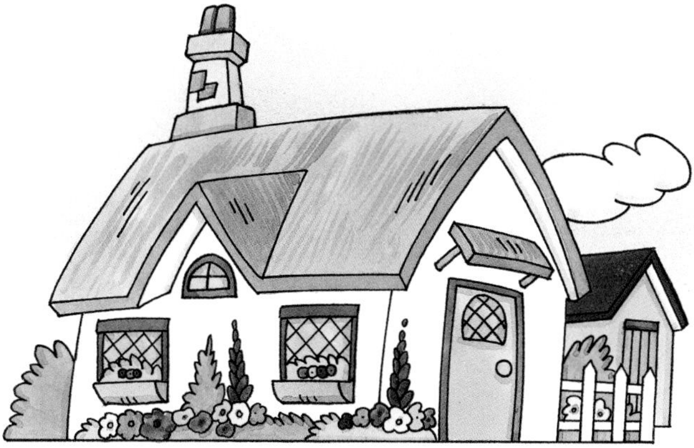

Illustrated by Kelvin Hawley

Rigby

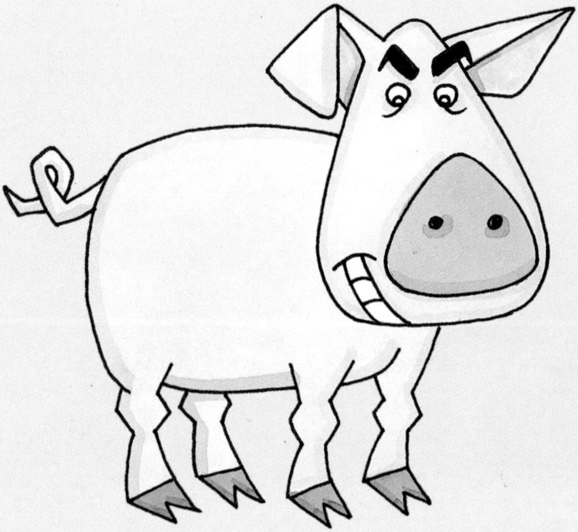

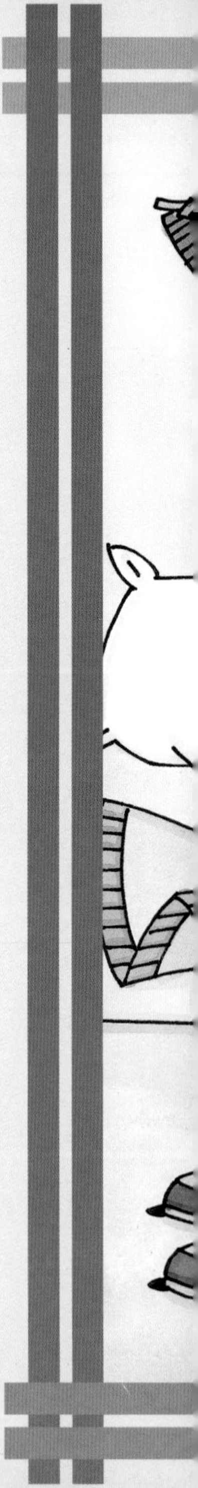

the pig

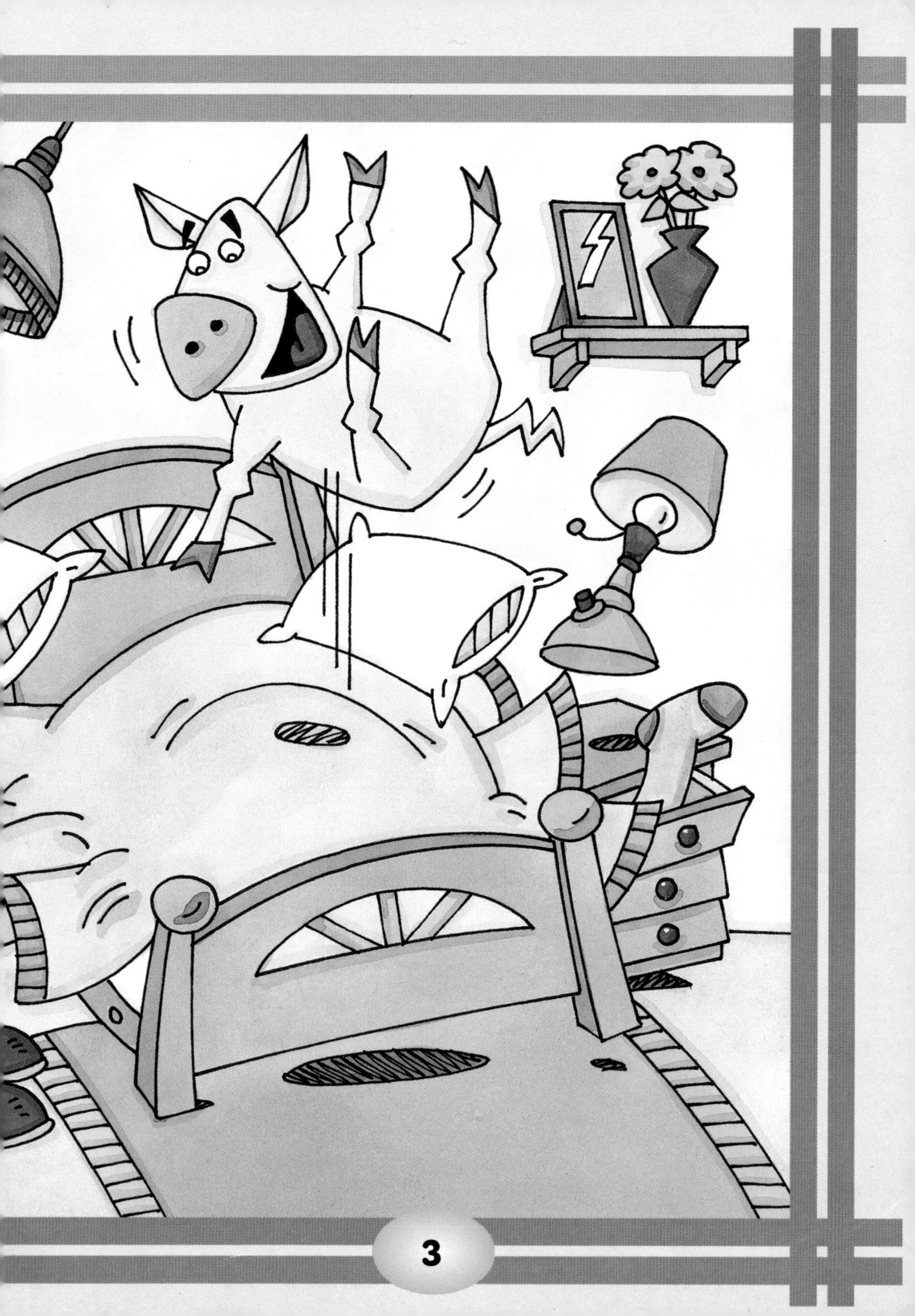

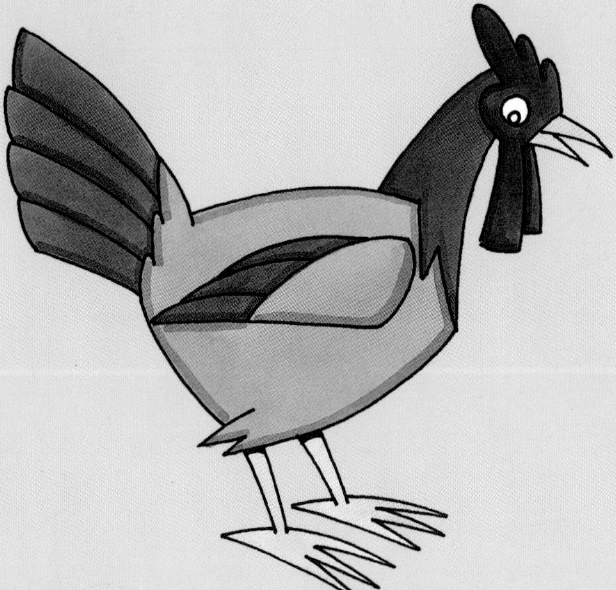

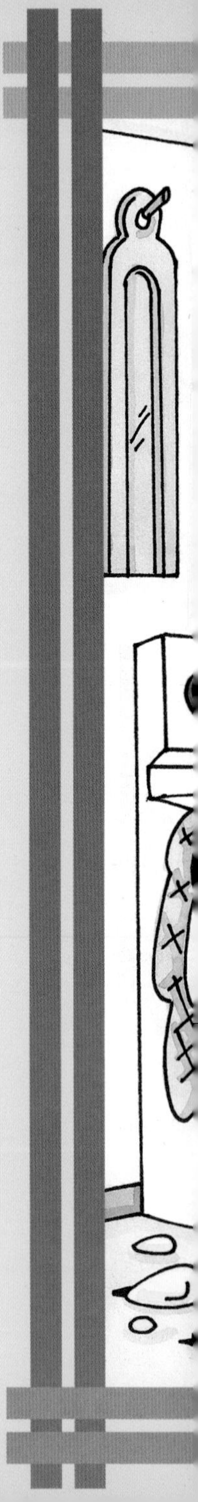

the hen

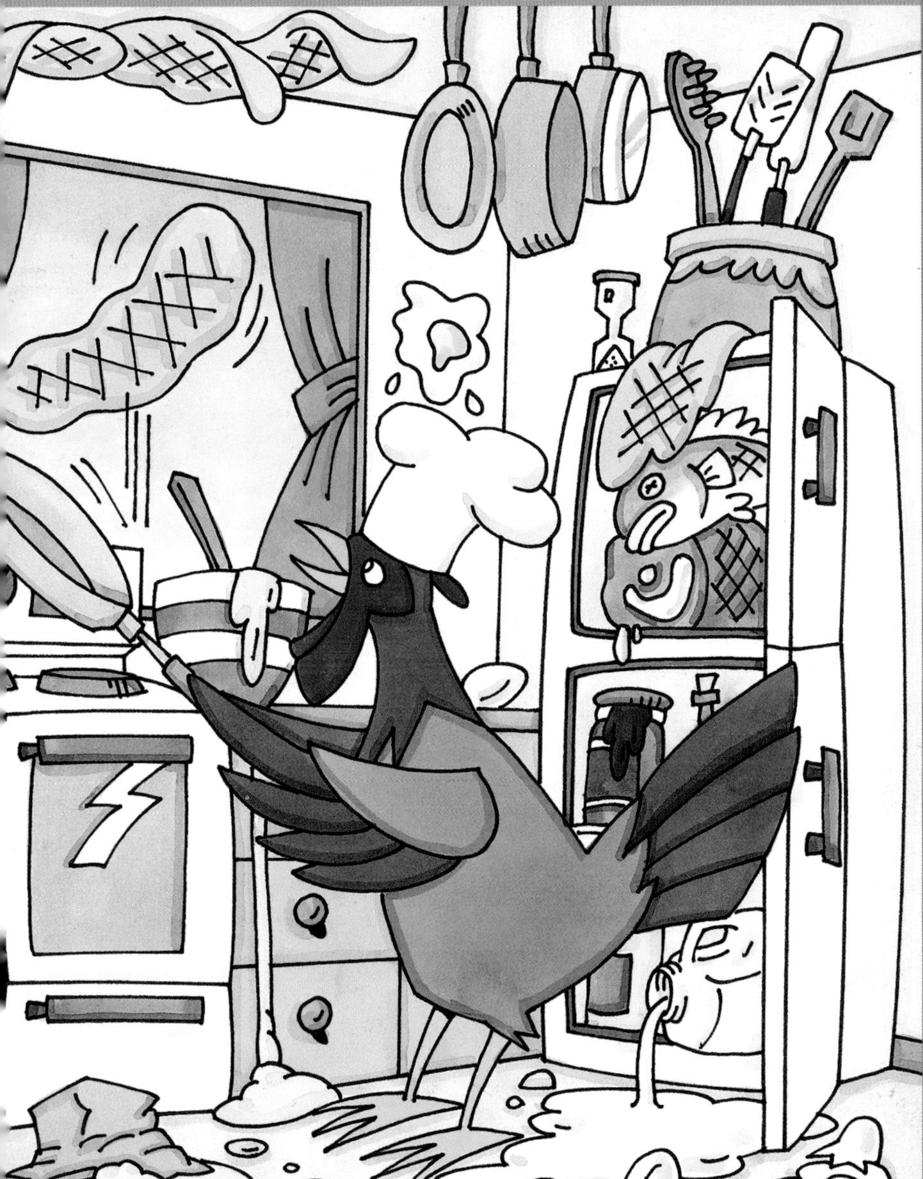

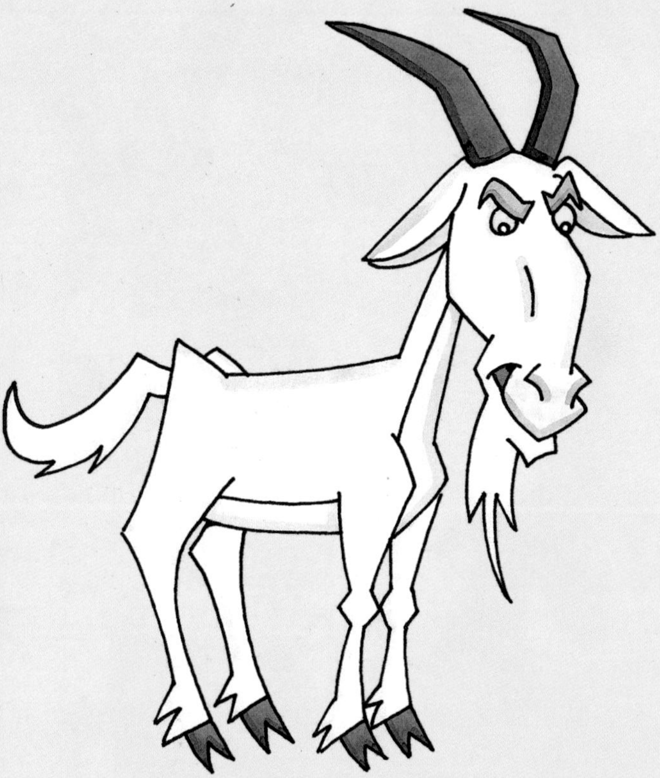

the goat

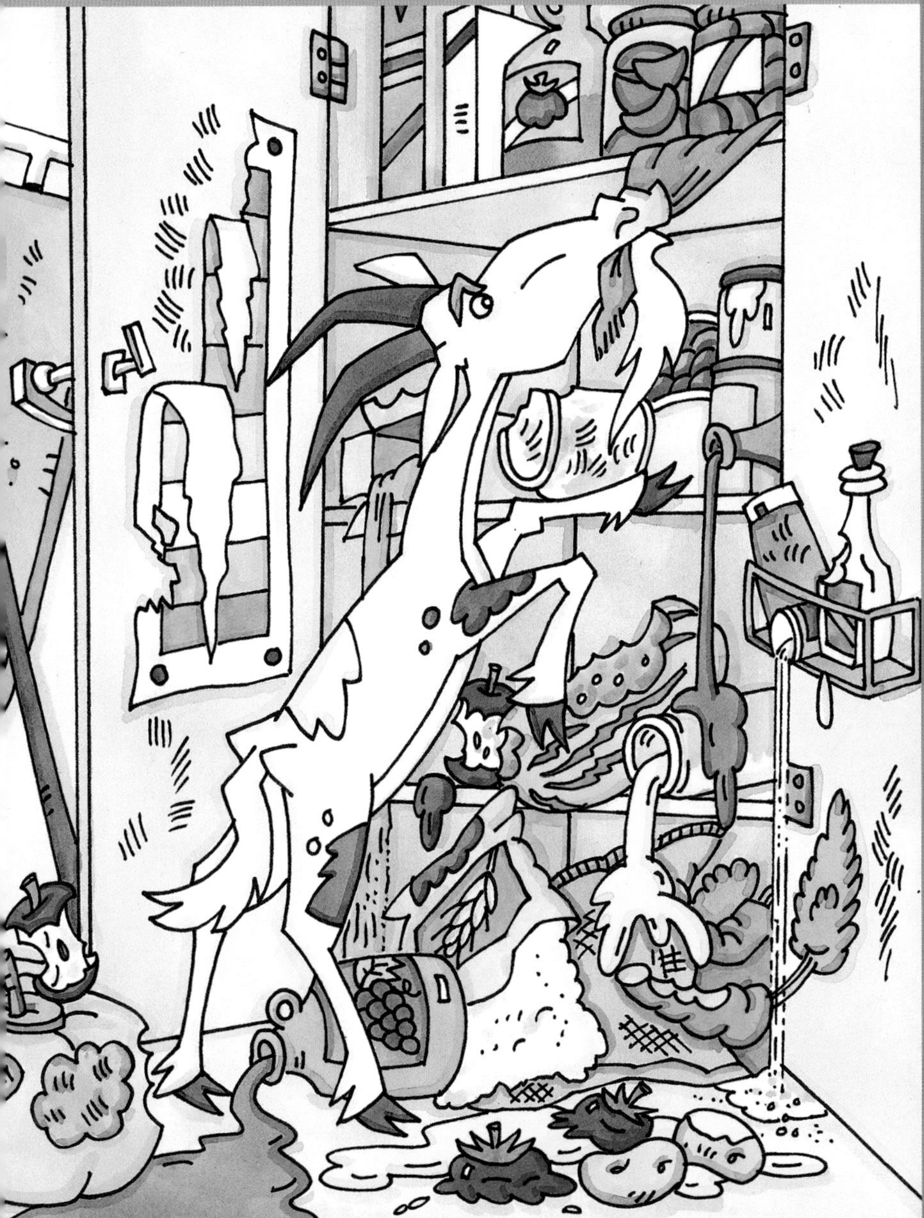

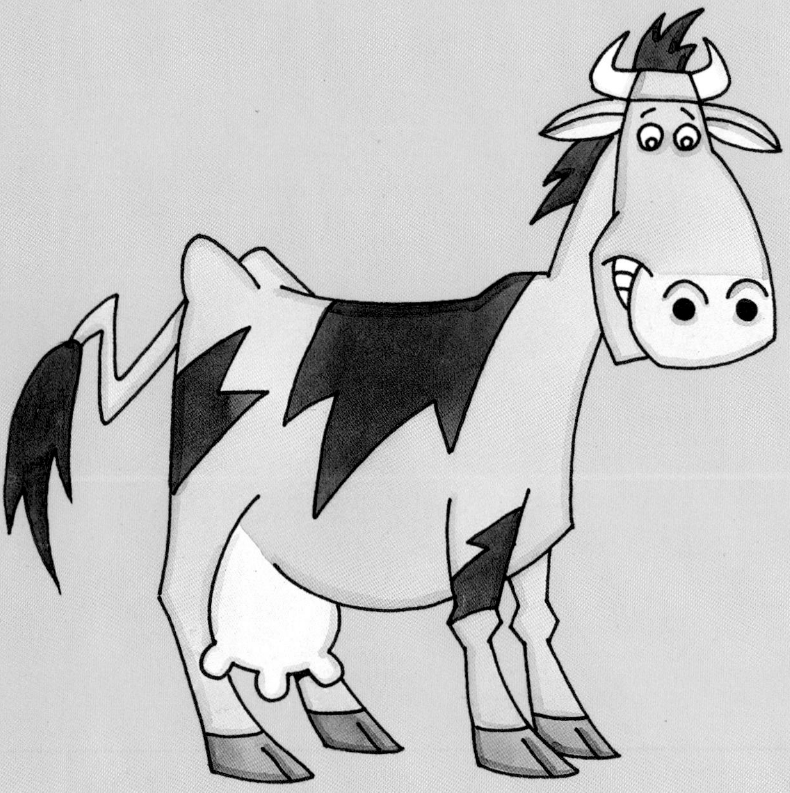

the cow

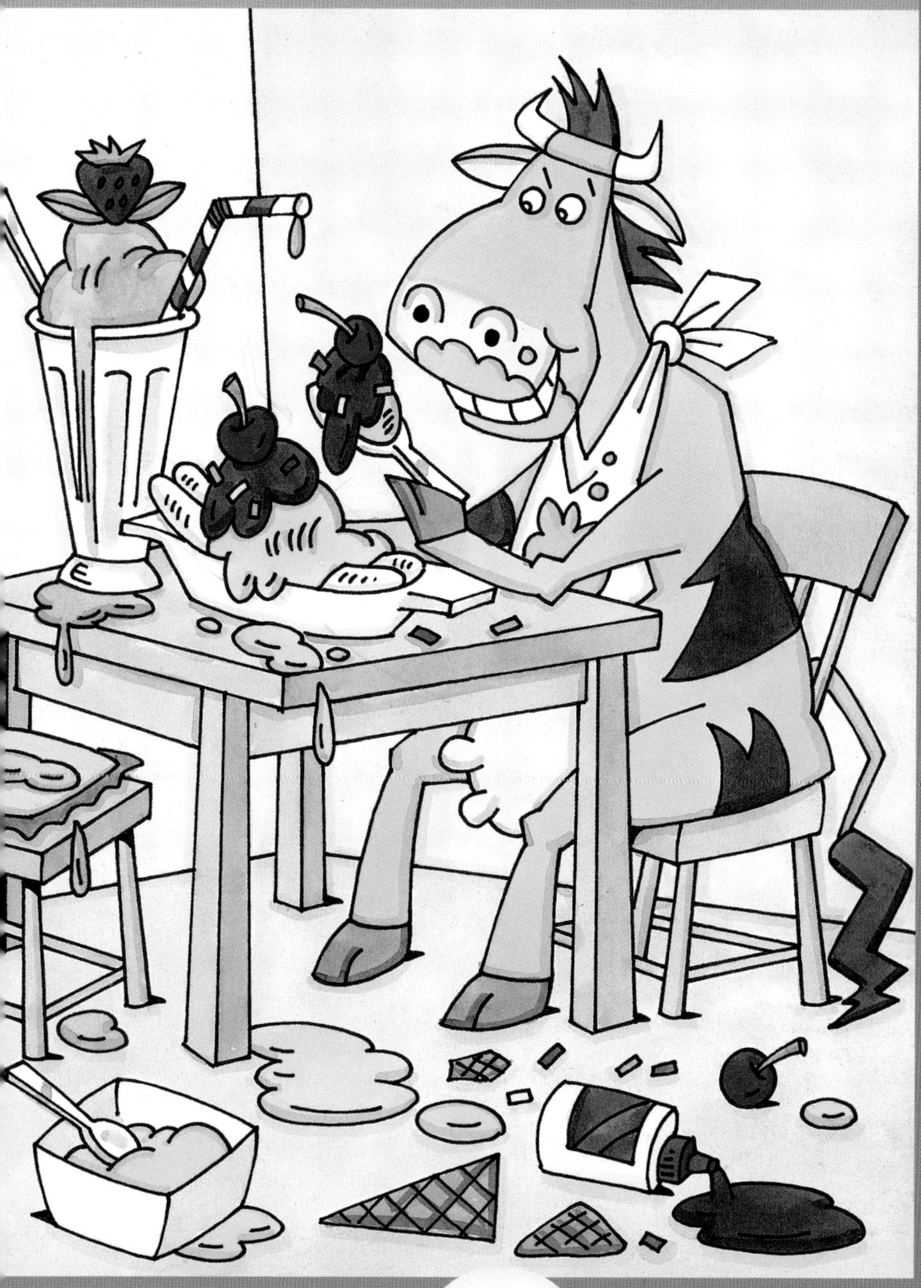

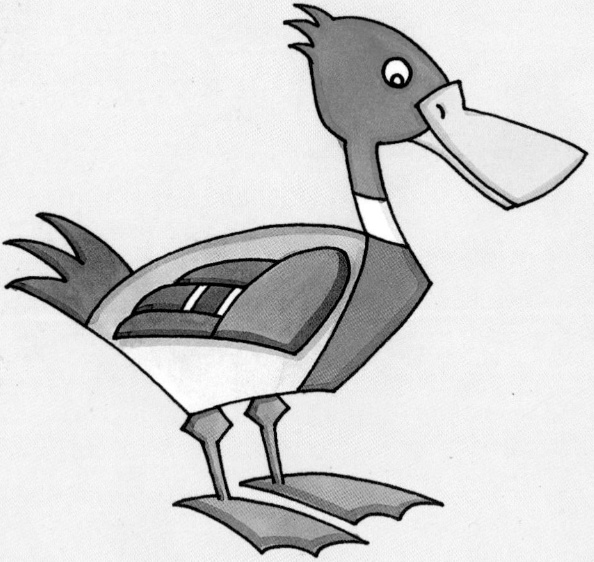

the duck

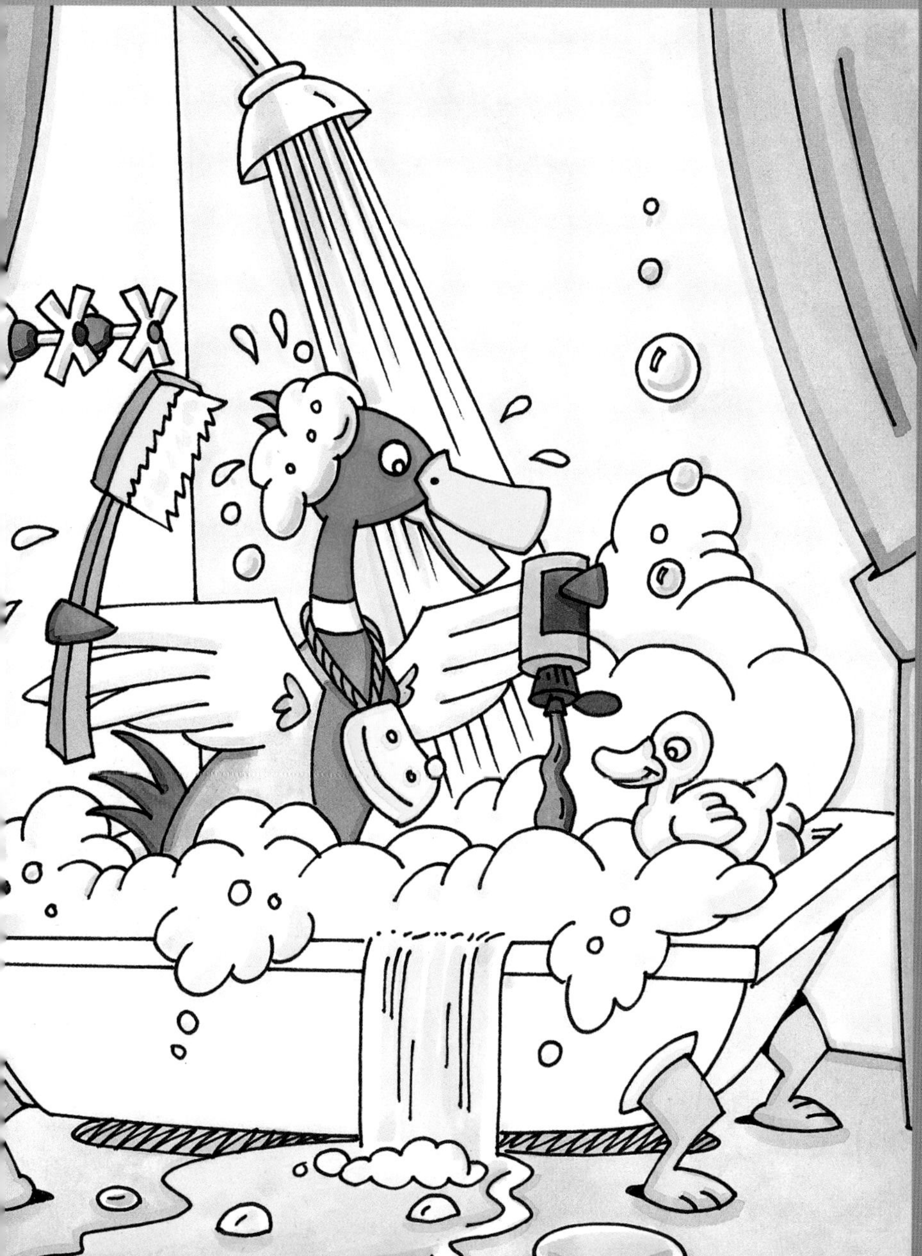

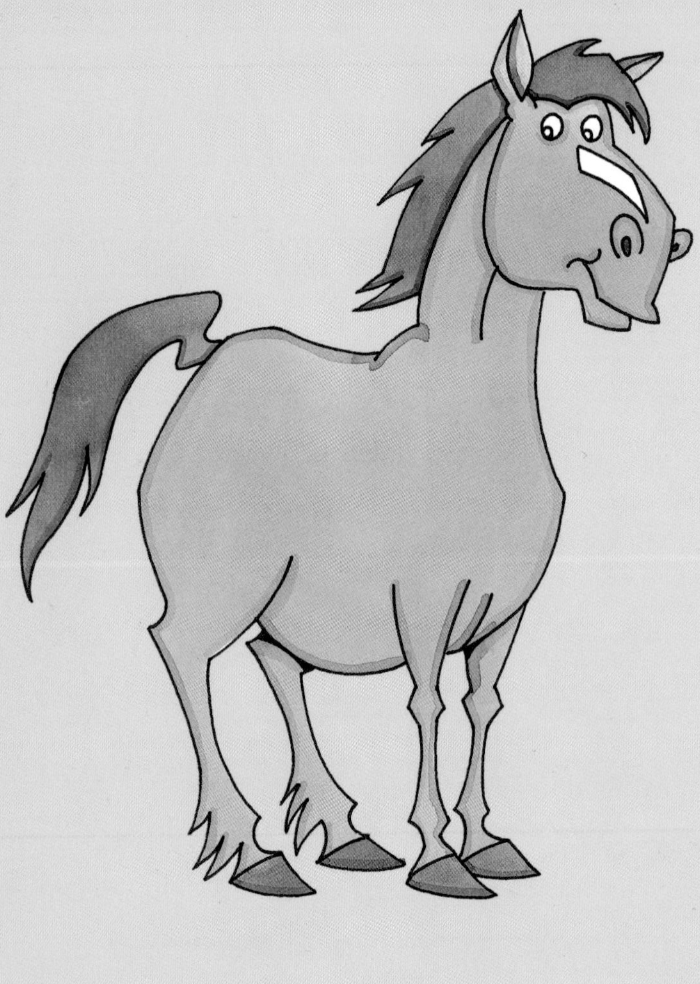

the horse

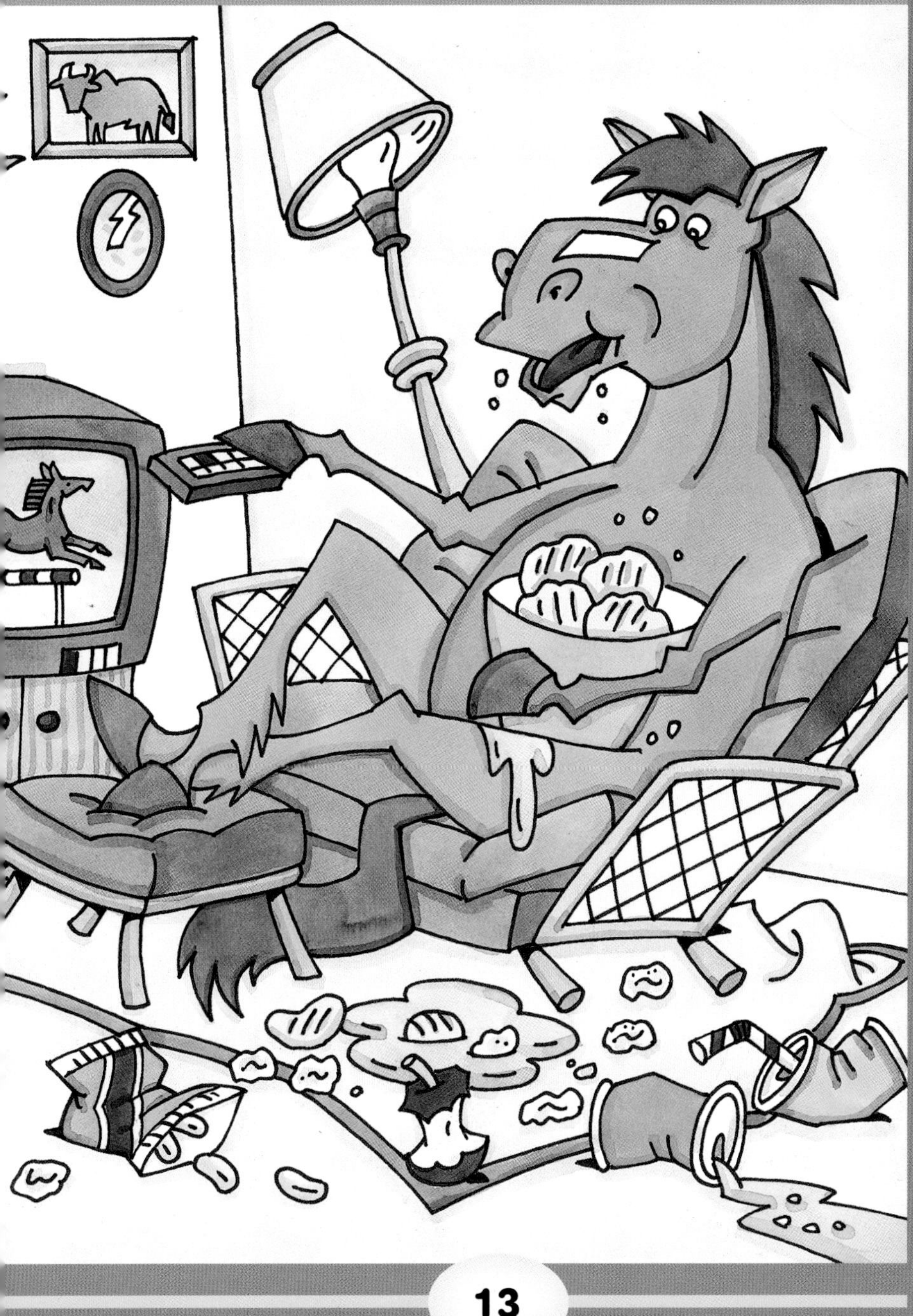

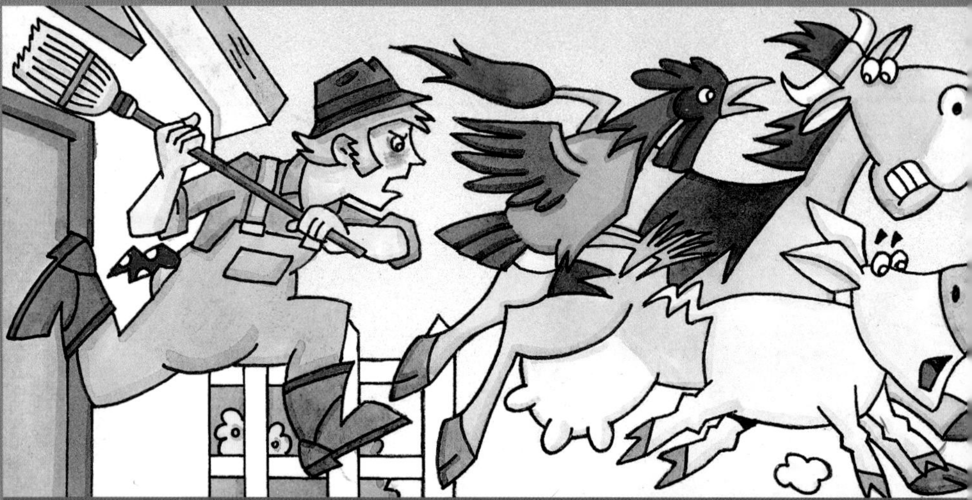

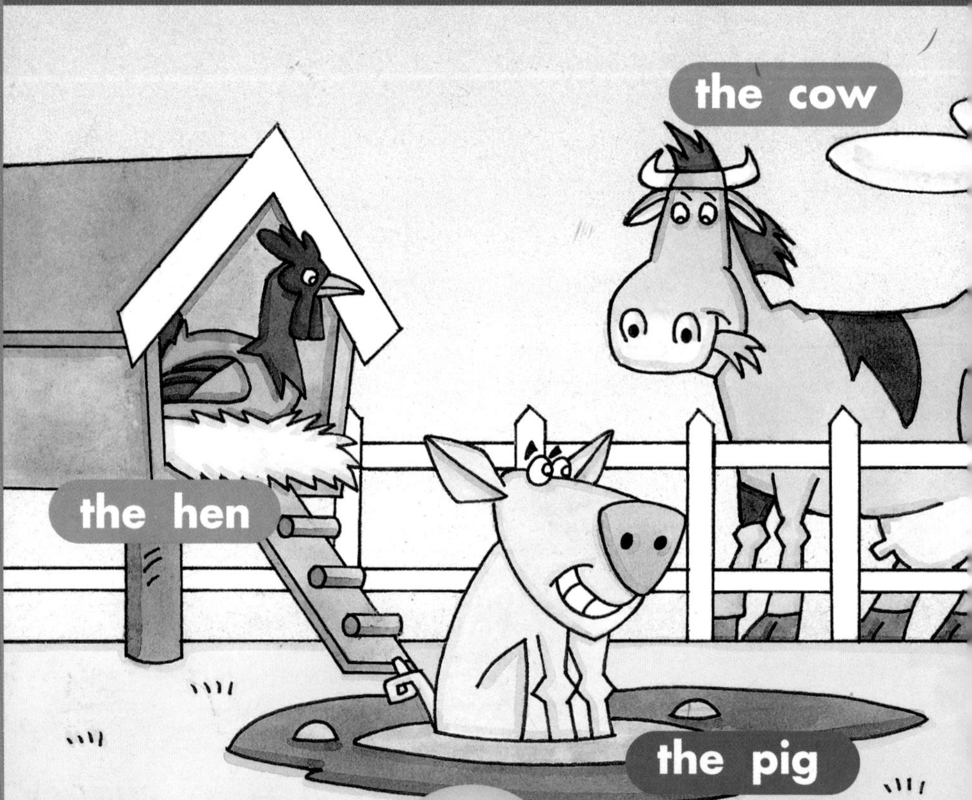
the cow
the hen
the pig

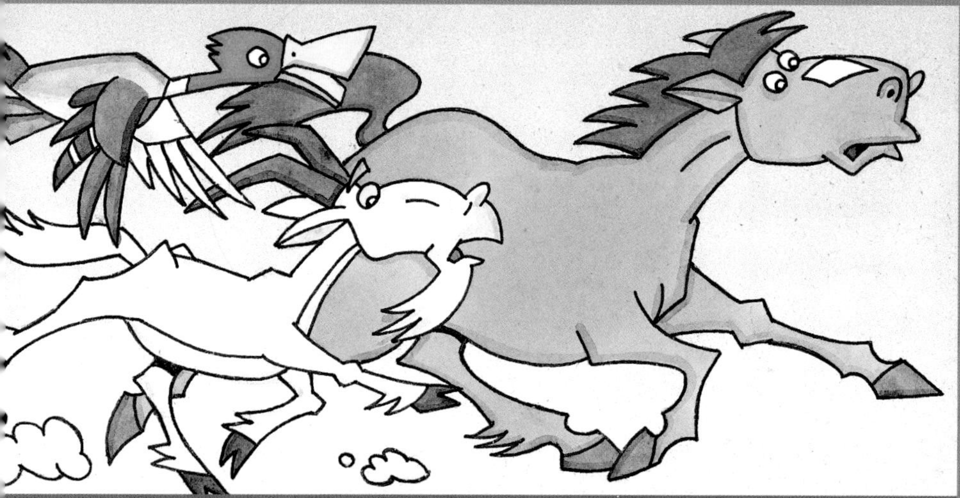

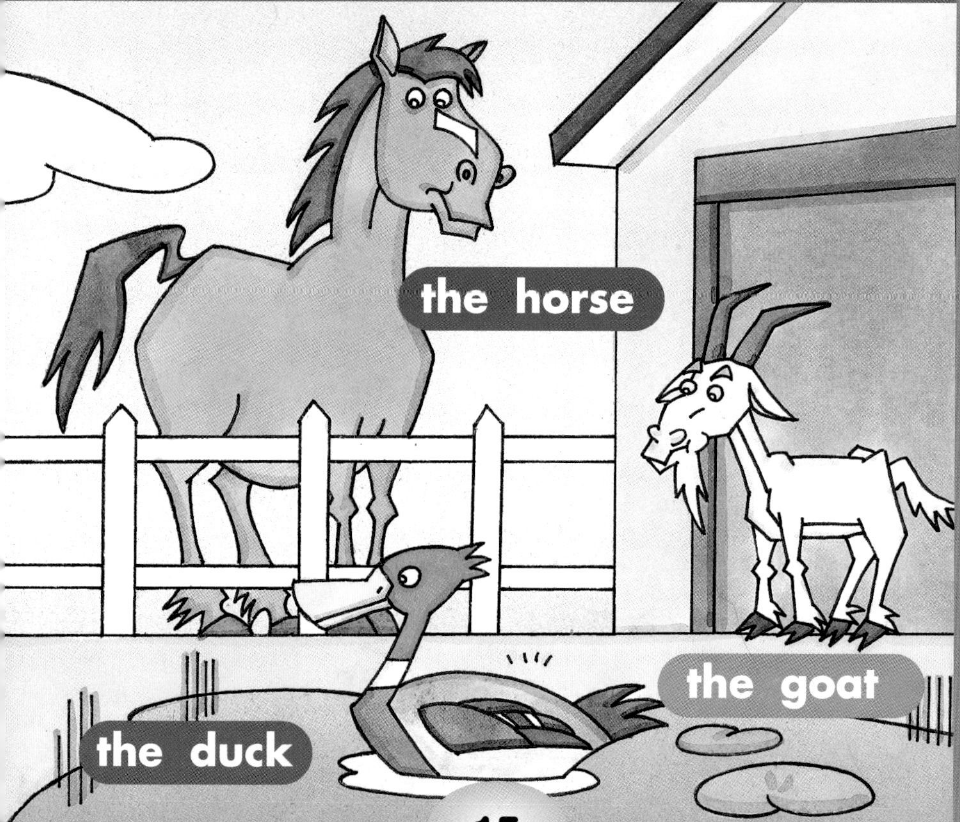
the horse
the goat
the duck

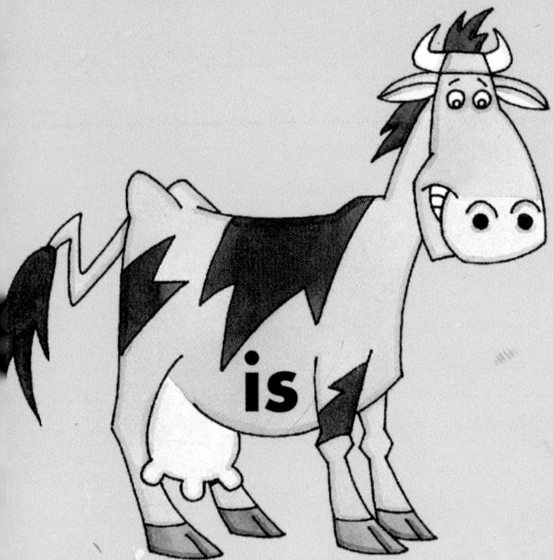
is

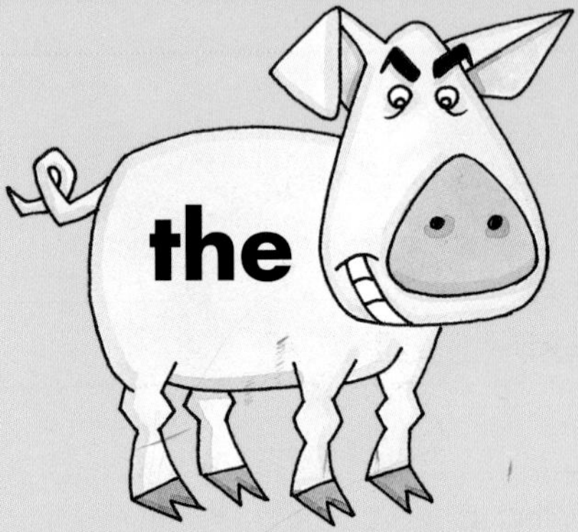
the

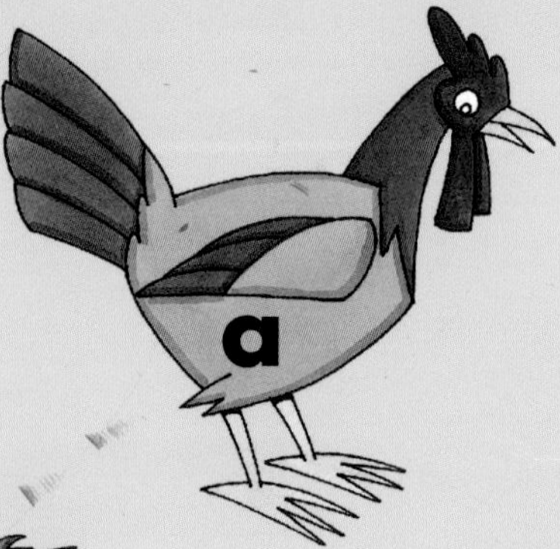
a

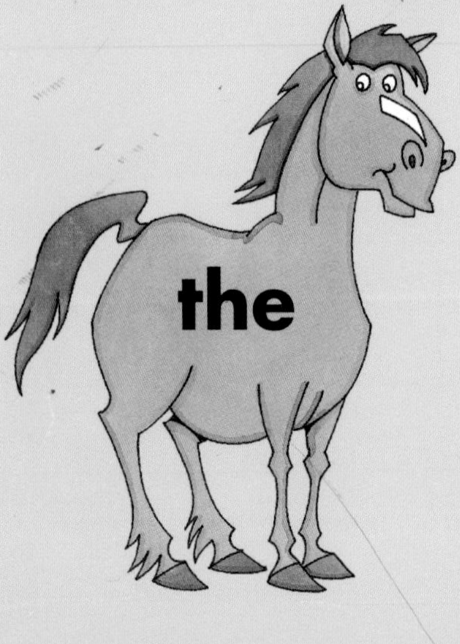
the

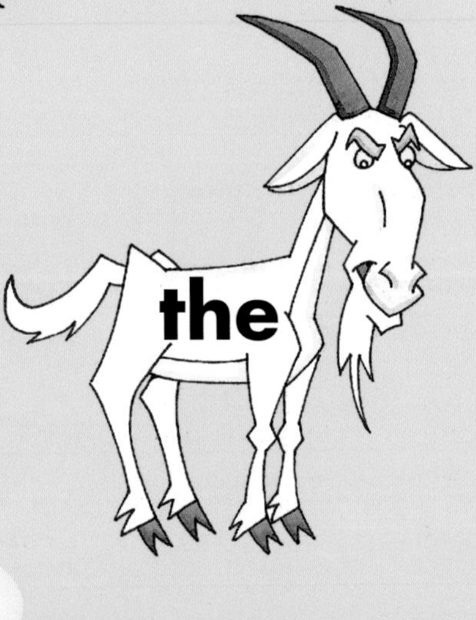
the